SCUOLA D'INGLESE

1° livello

S0-ARK-938

the adventures of Pinocchio

GIUNTI Junior

Geppetto is
a poor carpenter and
he has no children.
One day he takes
a strange
piece of wood
and makes a puppet.

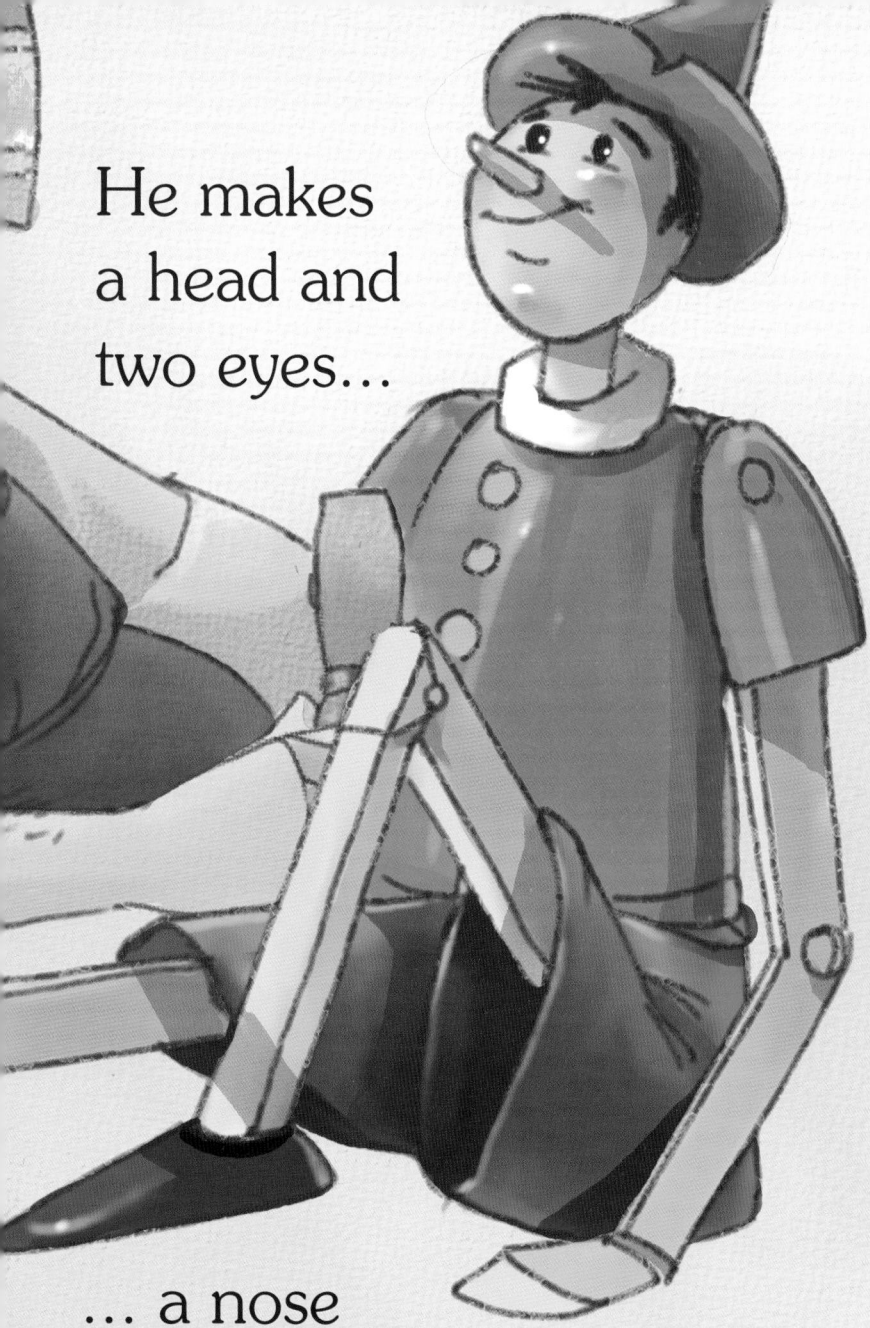

He makes
a head and
two eyes...

... a nose
and a mouth, two arms, two
hands, two legs and two feet.

Immediately the puppet
starts jumping around.
Geppetto is very happy.
The puppet is
his son now!

– You must go to school, but first you need a name – Geppetto says. – I can call you Pinocchio.

Geppetto goes out
and sells his coat
to buy a spelling
book.

At home Pinocchio hears a voice: – Hello, I'm Jiminy Cricket. Be good to Geppetto: he is a good man!

Geppetto gives Pinocchio the spelling book. – Go to school and be a good boy! Pinocchio leaves the house with his spelling book and...

... Jiminy Cricket follows him.

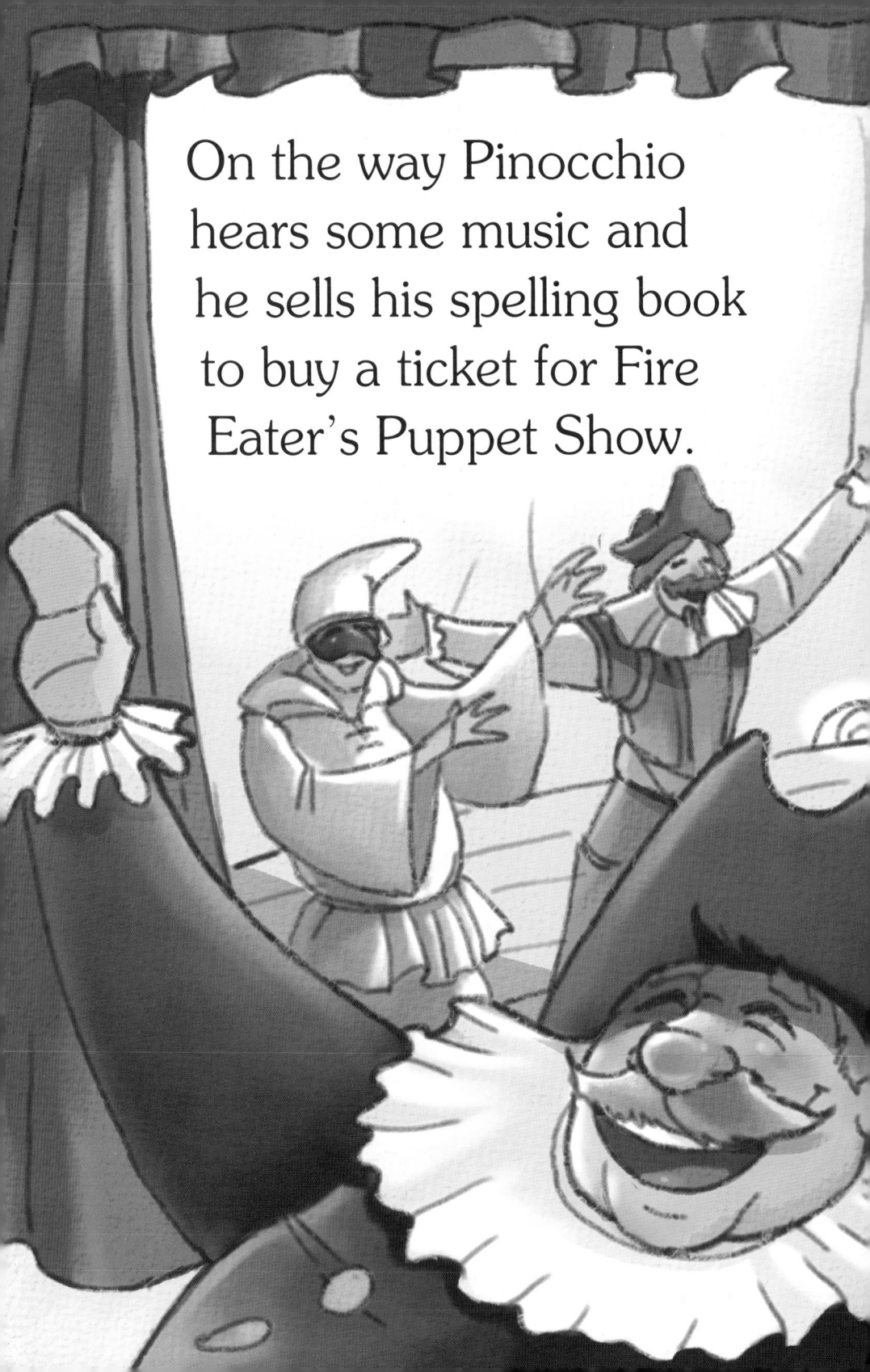

On the way Pinocchio hears some music and he sells his spelling book to buy a ticket for Fire Eater's Puppet Show.

Soon he is on stage
singing and dancing with
all the other puppets.

The show is a success and Fire Eater wants Pinocchio to stay.

– Remember that Geppetto wants you to go to school – says Jiminy Cricket.

Luckily Fire Eater knows Geppetto and gives Pinocchio five pieces of gold to take to him.

– I want to buy Geppetto a new coat with this money! – says Pinocchio.

On the way home he meets a cat and a fox and he tells them about his good fortune.
– You can make more money if you come with us – says the cat.

– Where? – asks Pinocchio.
– To our magic field – the fox says. – You bury the money and you have a tree of gold the next day.

– No, Pinocchio, that money is for Geppetto – cries Jiminy Cricket. But Pinocchio goes to the magic field and he buries the money.

The next day
he goes to the field but
there's no tree of gold.
There's only an empty
hole!

The money is not there!
He starts crying.

Near the field lives the Blue Fairy. She hears Pinocchio crying and she goes to see what is wrong.

– There's a hole in my pocket. The money I want to take to Geppetto is not here! – cries Pinocchio.

But suddenly his nose
begins to grow.
– Are you sure? Don't lie.
Where is your money? –
the Blue Fairy asks.

– I don't know. It's not
in my pocket anymore! –
replies Pinocchio.
His nose goes on growing.

The Blue Fairy laughs: – When you tell a lie your nose grows! So Pinocchio promises not to tell any more lies.

– Go home and be a good boy! – the Blue Fairy says. Pinocchio thanks the Fairy and runs home.

But on the way he meets a boy. – Come to the Land of Toys with me! – he says. – Nobody goes to school there and you can play all day long!

– Don't listen to him –
says Jiminy Cricket.

– We can take the carriage this evening – says the boy.

Pinocchio forgets all the promises to his father and to the Fairy. They jump up in the carriage to the Land of Toys.

– Life is great here!
No books, no lessons and
we can play all the time! –
cries Pinocchio.

One day Pinocchio
notices he has
long, hairy ears...

– You are turning into a donkey! – says Jiminy Cricket. – I want to go home! – cries Pinocchio.

– Jump into the sea
and escape from here! –
says Jiminy Cricket.

So they jump into the dark sea and swim in the waves.

Then they see a light
in the dark.

They swim and swim right into a whale's mouth.
– We are inside a whale! – cries Jiminy Cricket.

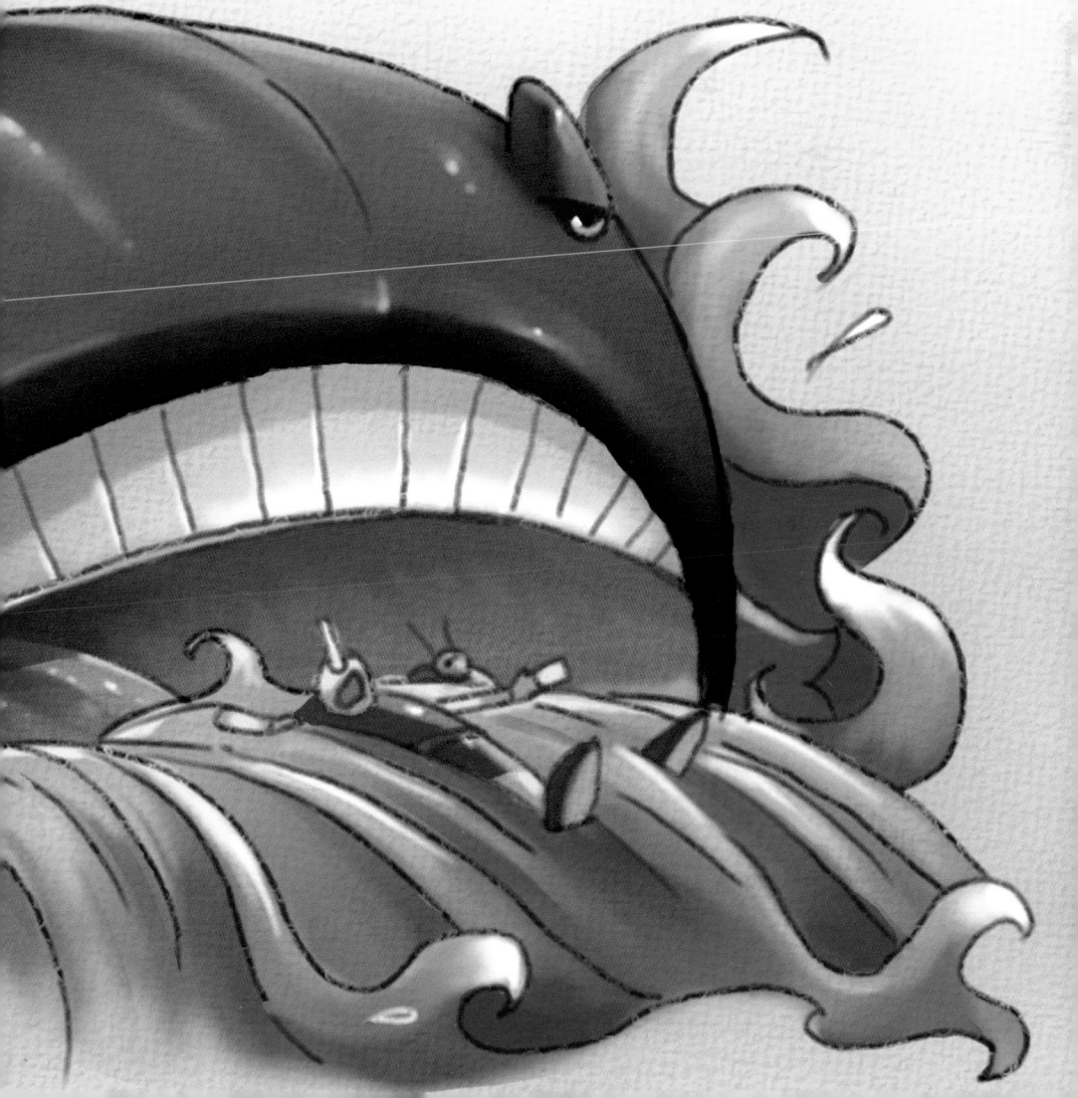

– Pinocchio! – a voice calls.
– What?! But it's you,
dad! – cries Pinocchio
so happy to see
Geppetto.

– We must get out of here
and swim to land! –
Pinocchio says.
When the whale opens its
mouth they get out.

Pinocchio swims and pulls Geppetto. When they reach dry land they are very tired.

Finally they
get home and
immediately fall asleep.

The next day they wake up and the Blue Fairy is there.
– Look in the mirror! – she says to Pinocchio.

Pinocchio is a real boy with blue eyes and brown hair.
– Oh, my son! – cries Geppetto with joy.

– You are a good boy:
this is your reward! –
says the Blue Fairy.

Pinocchio and Geppetto are very happy and they jump and laugh together!

TRADUZIONE

INGLESE / ITALIANO

Pagina 2

Geppetto is a poor carpenter and he has no children.
One day he takes a strange piece of wood and makes a puppet.

Geppetto è un falegname povero e senza figli.
Un giorno prende uno strano pezzo di legno e costruisce un burattino.

Pagina 3

He makes a head and two eyes, a nose and a mouth, two arms, two hands, two legs and two feet.

Costruisce una testa e due occhi, un naso e una bocca, due braccia, due mani, due gambe e due piedi.

Pagina 4

Immediately the puppet starts jumping around.
Geppetto is very happy. The puppet is his son now!

Immediatamente il burattino comincia a saltare tutt'intorno.
Geppetto è molto felice. Il burattino è suo figlio ora!

Pagina 5

– You must go to school, but first you need a name – Geppetto says.

– I can call you Pinocchio.

– Devi andare a scuola, ma prima hai bisogno di un nome – dice Geppetto. – Ti posso chiamare Pinocchio.

Pagina 6

Geppetto goes out and sells his coat to buy a spelling book.

Geppetto esce e vende la sua giacca per comprare un abbecedario.

Pagina 7

At home Pinocchio hears a voice: – Hello, I'm Jiminy Cricket. Be good to Geppetto: he is a good man!

A casa Pinocchio sente una voce: – Ciao, sono il Grillo Parlante. Sii buono con Geppetto: è un brav'uomo!

Pagina 8

Geppetto gives Pinocchio the spelling book. – Go to school and be a good boy!
Pinocchio leaves the house with his spelling book and...

Geppetto dà a Pinocchio il suo abbecedario. – Vai a scuola e fai il bravo! Pinocchio esce di casa con l'abbecedario e...

Pagina 9

... Jiminy Cricket follows him.

... il Grillo Parlante lo segue.

Pagina 10

On the way Pinocchio hears some music and he sells his spelling book to buy a ticket for Fire Eater's Puppet Show.

Per la strada Pinocchio sente della musica e vende il suo abbecedario per comprare un biglietto per lo spettacolo di burattini di Mangiafuoco.

Pagina 11

Soon he is on stage singing and dancing with all the other puppets.

Presto è sul palco a cantare e a ballare con tutti gli altri burattini.

Pagina 12

The show is a success and Fire Eater wants Pinocchio to stay.

Lo spettacolo è un successo e Mangiafuoco vuole che Pinocchio resti.

Pagina 13

– Remember that Geppetto wants you to go to school – says Jiminy Cricket.

– Ricorda che Geppetto vuole che tu vada a scuola – dice il Grillo Parlante.

Pagina 14

Luckily Fire Eater knows Geppetto and gives Pinocchio five pieces of gold to take to him.

Per fortuna Mangiafuoco conosce Geppetto e dà a Pinocchio cinque monete d'oro da portargli.

Pagina 15

– I want to buy Geppetto a new coat with this money! – says Pinocchio.

– Voglio comprare a Geppetto una giacca nuova con questi soldi! – dice Pinocchio.

Pagina 16

On the way home he meets a cat and a fox and he tells them about his good fortune. – You can make more money if you come with us – says the cat.

Lungo la strada di casa incontra un gatto e una volpe e racconta loro della sua buona sorte. – Puoi fare più soldi se vieni con noi – dice il gatto.

Pagina 17

– Where? – asks Pinocchio. – To our magic field – the fox says. – You bury the money and you have a tree of gold the next day.

– Dove? – chiede Pinocchio. – Nel nostro campo magico – dice la volpe. – Si sotterra il denaro e il giorno dopo trovi un albero d'oro.

Pagina 18

– No, Pinocchio, that money is for Geppetto – cries Jiminy Cricket.
But Pinocchio goes to the magic field and he buries the money.

– No, Pinocchio, quei soldi sono per Geppetto – grida il Grillo Parlante. Ma Pinocchio va al campo magico e sotterra il denaro.

Pagina 19

The next day he goes to the field but there's no tree of gold.
There's only an empty hole!

Il giorno dopo ritorna al campo ma non c'è nessun albero d'oro.
C'è solo una buca vuota!

Pagina 20

The money is not there! He starts crying.

Il denaro non c'è! Inizia a piangere.

Pagina 21

Near the field lives the Blue Fairy.
She hears Pinocchio crying and she goes to see what is wrong.

Vicino al campo vive la Fata Turchina.
Sente piangere Pinocchio e va a vedere cos'è che non va.

Pagina 22

– There's a hole in my pocket. The money I want to take to Geppetto is not here! – cries Pinocchio.

– C'è un buco nella mia tasca. I soldi che voglio portare a Geppetto non ci sono! – piange Pinocchio.

Pagina 23

But suddenly his nose begins to grow.
– Are you sure? Don't lie. Where is your money? – the Blue Fairy asks.

Ma improvvisamente il suo naso comincia a crescere.
– Sei sicuro? Non mentire. Dove sono i soldi? – chiede la Fata Turchina.

Pagina 24

– I don't know. It's not in my pocket anymore! – replies Pinocchio.
His nose goes on growing.

– Non lo so. Non sono più nella mia tasca! – replica Pinocchio.
Il suo naso continua a crescere.

Pagina 25

The Blue Fairy laughs: – When you tell a lie your nose grows!
So Pinocchio promises not to tell any more lies.

La Fata Turchina sorride: – Quando dici una bugia il tuo naso cresce!
Così Pinocchio promette di non raccontare più bugie.

Pagina 26

– Go home and be a good boy! – the Blue Fairy says.
Pinocchio thanks the Fairy and runs home.

– Vai a casa e sii buono! – dice la Fata Turchina.
Pinocchio ringrazia la Fata e corre a casa.

Pagina 27

But on the way he meets a boy. – Come to the Land of Toys with me! – he says. – Nobody goes to school there and you can play all day long!

Ma lungo la strada incontra un ragazzo. – Vieni con me nel Paese dei Balocchi! – dice. – Nessuno va a scuola lì e si può giocare tutto il giorno!

Pagina 28

– Don't listen to him – says Jiminy Cricket.

– Non ascoltarlo – dice il Grillo Parlante.

Pagina 29

– We can take the carriage this evening – says the boy.

– Possiamo prendere la carrozza questa sera – dice il ragazzo.

Pagina 30

Pinocchio forgets all the promises to his father and to the Fairy.
They jump up in the carriage to the Land of Toys.

Pinocchio dimentica tutte le promesse fatte a suo padre e alla Fata.
Saltano nella carrozza verso il Paese dei Balocchi.

Pagina 31

– Life is great here! No books, no lessons and we can play all the time! – cries Pinocchio.

– La vita qui è meravigliosa! Niente libri, niente lezioni e possiamo giocare tutto il tempo! – esclama Pinocchio.

Pagina 32

One day Pinocchio notices he has long, hairy ears...

Un giorno Pinocchio si accorge di avere delle lunghe orecchie pelose...

Pagina 33

– You are turning into a donkey! – says Jiminy Cricket.
– I want to go home! – cries Pinocchio.

– Ti stai trasformando in un asinello! – dice il Grillo Parlante.
– Voglio tornare a casa! – piange Pinocchio.

Pagina 34

– Jump into the sea and escape from here! – says Jiminy Cricket.

– Buttati in mare e scappa di qui! – dice il Grillo Parlante.

Pagina 35

So they jump into the dark sea and swim in the waves.

Così si tuffano nel mare scuro e nuotano tra le onde.

Pagina 36

Then they see a light in the dark.

Poi vedono una luce nel buio.

Pagina 37

They swim and swim right into a whale's mouth.
– We are inside a whale! – cries Jiminy Cricket.

Nuotano e nuotano proprio dentro la bocca di una balena.
– Siamo dentro a una balena! – grida il Grillo Parlante.

Pagina 38

– Pinocchio! – a voice calls. – What?! But it's you, dad! – cries Pinocchio so happy to see Geppetto.

– Pinocchio! – una voce chiama. – Cosa?! Ma sei tu, babbo! – grida Pinocchio così felice di vedere Geppetto.

Pagina 39

– We must get out of here and swim to land! – Pinocchio says.
When the whale opens its mouth they get out.

– Dobbiamo uscire da qui e nuotare verso terra! – dice Pinocchio.
Quando la balena apre la bocca escono fuori.

Pagina 40

Pinocchio swims and pulls Geppetto.
When they reach dry land they are very tired.

Pinocchio nuota e tira Geppetto.
Quando raggiungono la terraferma sono molto stanchi.

Pagina 41

Finally they get home and immediately fall asleep.

Alla fine arrivano a casa e si addormentano immediatamente.

Pagina 42

The next day they wake up and the Blue Fairy is there.
– Look in the mirror! – she says to Pinocchio.

Il mattino seguente si svegliano e la Fata Turchina è lì.
– Guardati allo specchio! – dice a Pinocchio.

Pagina 43

Pinocchio is a real boy with blue eyes and brown hair.
– Oh, my son! – cries Geppetto with joy.

Pinocchio è un bambino vero con gli occhi blu e i capelli marroni.
– Oh, figlio mio! – esclama Geppetto con gioia.

Pagina 44

– You are a good boy: this is your reward! – says the Blue Fairy.

– Sei un bravo bambino: questo è il tuo premio! – dice la Fata Turchina.

Pagina 45

Pinocchio and Geppetto are very happy and they jump and laugh together!

Pinocchio e Geppetto sono molto felici e saltano e ridono insieme!

Short summary

 makes a  out of a piece of  . The puppet is alive and Geppetto gives him a spelling  to go to  .

 sells the spelling book to buy a  for a puppet show. Fire Eater gives Pinocchio some 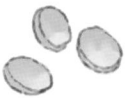 to take to Geppetto. But Pinocchio tells a  and a  about his good fortune. They take

Pinocchio to a Magic  and he buries the money. The next day the money is gone. The Blue  arrives and Pinocchio lies to her, so his  begins to grow very long. On the way home he meets a  and he follows him to the Land of Toys. Here Pinocchio starts growing long  like a  . He runs away and jumps into the  . He swims inside a 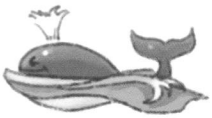 and meets Geppetto.They arrive home and the Blue Fairy turns Pinocchio into a real  .

Find the Differences

Look carefully at the two pictures and find the 5 differences.

Osserva attentamente le due immagini e trova le 5 differenze.

A Wordsearch

Find 4 words of the story!

Trova 4 parole della storia!

FOX **CAT**

WHALE **PUPPET**

A	P	I	L	V	P
Y	F	O	X	C	U
U	B	N	A	K	P
H	T	J	C	D	P
S	W	H	A	L	E
Z	G	W	T	E	T
R	Q	O	X	F	M

What is this?

Join the numbers from one to eighteen!

Unisci i numeri dall'uno al diciotto!

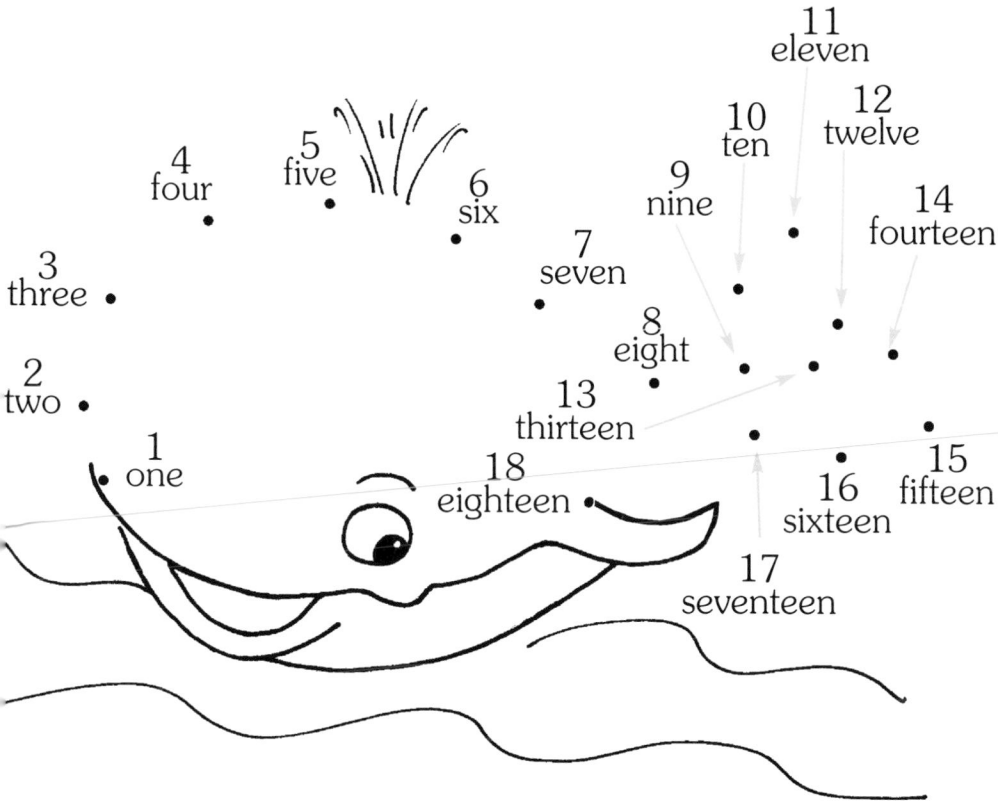

THIS IS A W _ _ _ _

IN THE SEA!

Match the Word with the picture!

BLUE FAIRY

PINOCCHIO

FIRE EATER

GEPPETTO

A Crossword

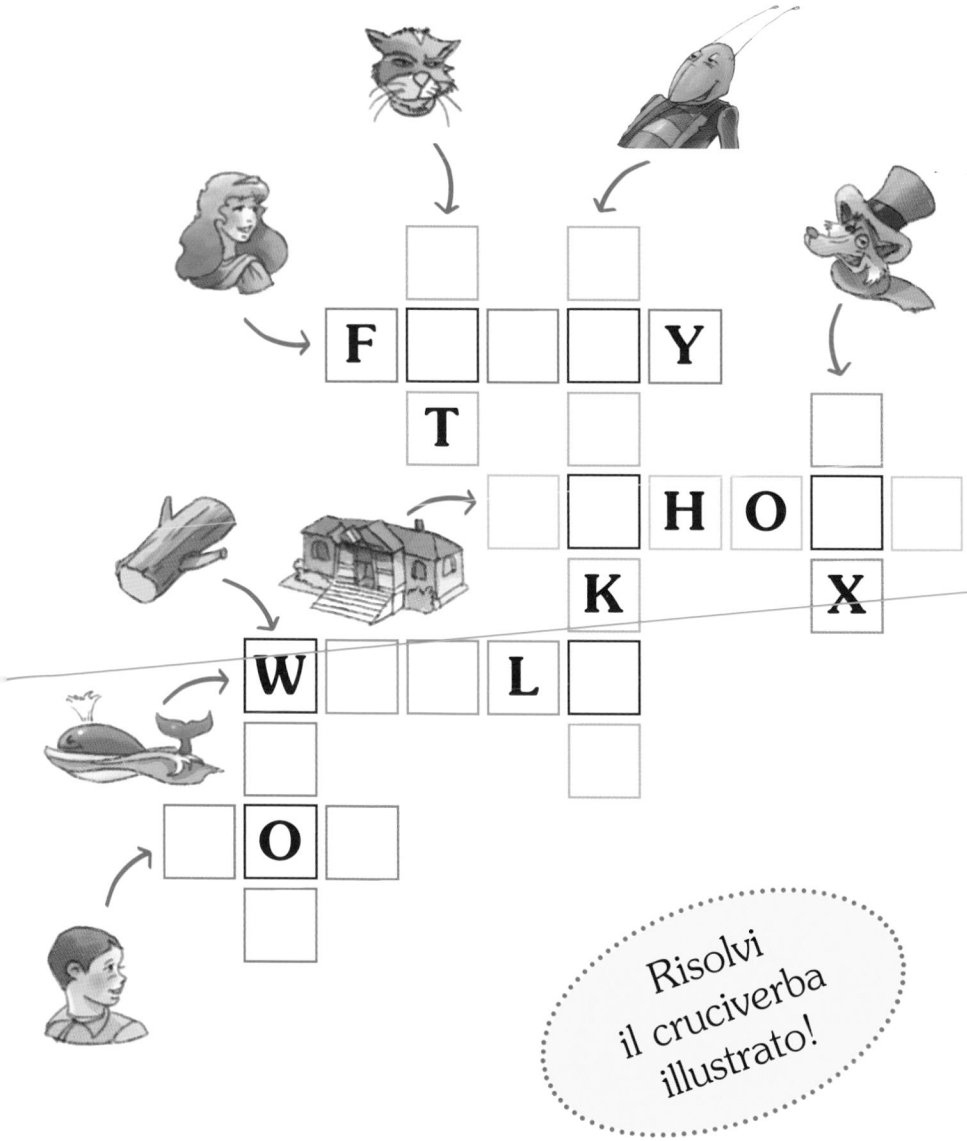

Risolvi il cruciverba illustrato!

A Maze

Help Pinocchio to reach
the carriage to the Land of Toys!

*Aiuta Pinocchio a raggiungere
la carrozza diretta al Paese dei Balocchi!*

A little dictionary

sostantivi

BOY: RAGAZZO
CARPENTER: FALEGNAME
CAT: GATTO
COAT: GIACCA
CRICKET: GRILLO
DONKEY: ASINO
FAIRY: FATA
FIELD: CAMPO
FOX: VOLPE
LIE: BUGIA
MOUTH: BOCCA
NOSE: NASO
POCKET: TASCA
PUPPET: BURATTINO
SCHOOL: SCUOLA
SON: FIGLIO
WHALE: BALENA
WOOD: LEGNO

aggettivi

EMPTY: VUOTO
GOOD: BUONO, BRAVO
HAIRY: PELOSO

HAPPY: FELICE
POOR: POVERO
TIRED: STANCO

• • • **verbi** • • •

to BURY: SOTTERRARE
to BUY: COMPRARE
to ESCAPE: SCAPPARE
to FOLLOW: SEGUIRE
to GIVE: DARE
to JUMP: SALTARE
to GROW: CRESCERE
to LIE: MENTIRE
to MAKE: FARE, COSTRUIRE
to MEET: INCONTRARE
to PLAY: GIOCARE
to SELL: VENDERE
to SWIM: NUOTARE

A cura di Gabriella Ballarin • Illustrazioni: Giulio Peranzoni
Progetto grafico: Romina Ferrari • Impaginazione: Simonetta Zuddas

www.giunti.it

© 2007 Giunti Editore S.p.A.
Via Bolognese, 165 - 50139 Firenze - Italia
Via Dante, 4 - 20121 Milano - Italia

Prima edizione: maggio 2007

Ristampa	Anno
7 6 5 4 3 2	2014 2013 2012 2011 2010

Stampato presso Giunti Industrie Grafiche S.p.A. – Stabilimento di Prato